HELPING POL PARROT!

Pirates Can Be Kind

Written by
Tom Easton

Illustrated by
Mike Gordon

WAYLAND

Polly parrot was down in
the beak. She loved being a pirate
parrot, but sometimes life on board
ship was quite hard.

HELPING POLLY PARROT!

Pir tes Can Be Kind

Published in paperback in 2015 by Wayland
Text copyright © Wayland 2015
Illustrations copyright © Mike Gordon
All rights reserved.

Dewey Number: 823.9'2-dc23
ISBN: 978 0 7502 8926 9
Ebook ISBN: 978 0 7502 8555 1

Wayland, an imprint of
Hachette Children's Group
Part of Hodder & Stoughton
Carmelite House
50 Victoria Embankment
London EC4Y 0DZ

10 9 8 7 6 5 4 3 2 1

Commissioning editor: Victoria Brooker
Creative design: Basement68

One of the main problems was
that Polly had nowhere to sleep.
The captain had his cot bed.

She had tried to perch on the top of it,
but his night-light kept her awake.

She tried to snuggle in with Nell once, but Polly's beak was too sharp and Nell shooed her away.

The boys' cabin was too noisy (and smelly).

She tried to sleep above deck, but everywhere
she perched she'd end up in someone's way.
"Don't sit on that!" Nell shouted.

"Out the way, Polly," Davy called.
"Squawk off!" Pete cried.

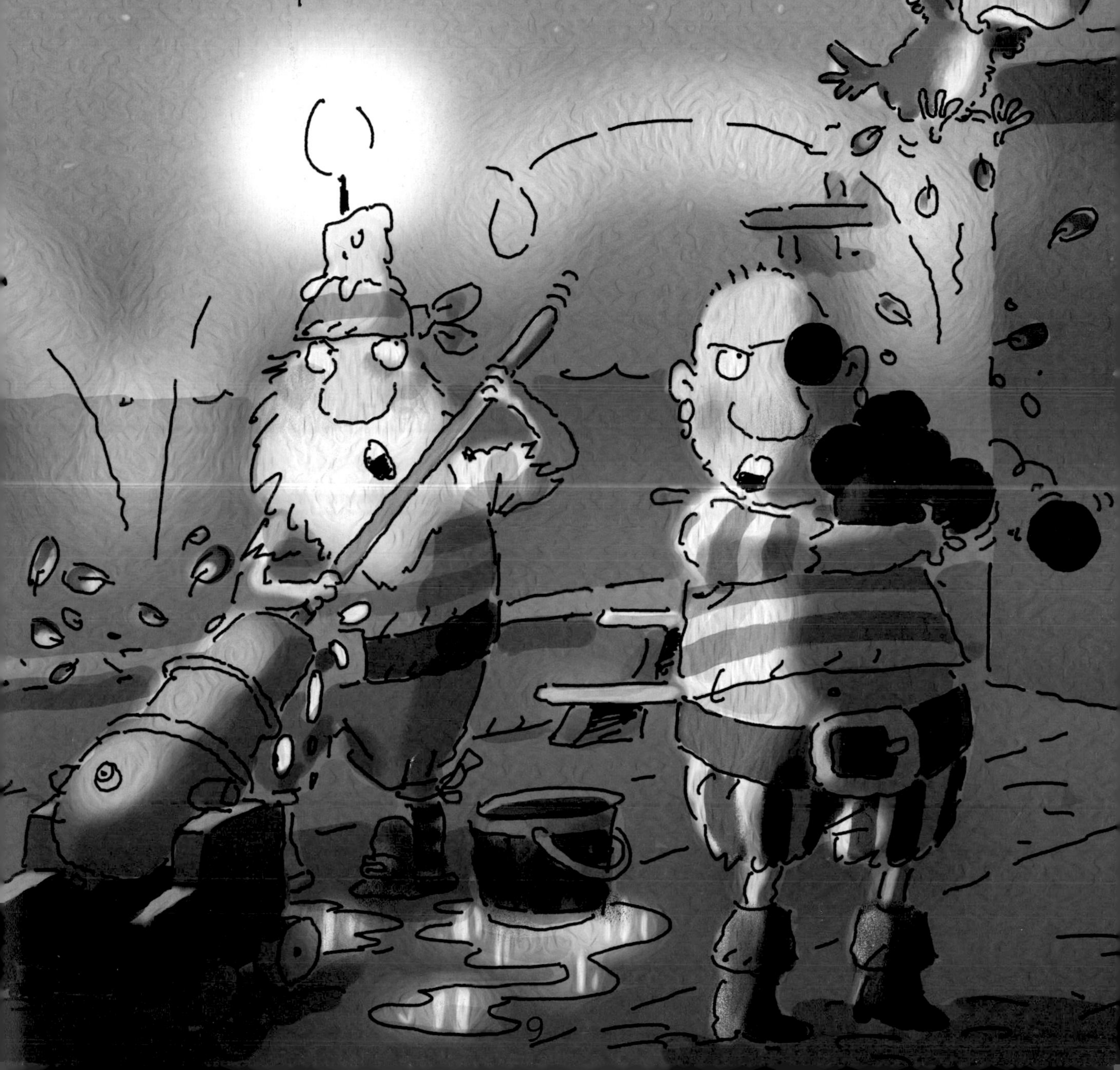

One night, Polly flew to the top of the tallest mast of the ship, out of everyone's way. But that night was cold. That night was wet. That night was windy.

Sam shivered in the crow's nest
nearby, keeping watch.
"Poor old Polly," he muttered.

The next morning, the sun came out!
It was Polly's turn to be look-out and she
sighed happily in the crow's nest, warming her
feathers. Soon enough, she dropped off to
sleep, dreaming of cheese and crackers.

But oh no! While Polly slept, the *Golden Duck*
was heading towards a rocky island!
Closer and closer they came to the cruel
and jagged rocks, until....

"Rocks!" came a cry. Luckily Nell had noticed they were headed towards danger.

The Captain spun the wheel
and the *Golden Duck* swept past
the island with just feet to spare.
They lost Sam's washing line,
but that was all.

"Why didn't you warn us?!" Pete shouted. "We nearly hit those rocks because of you," Davy said, shaking his head.

"I've lost my favourite pair of bloomers," Nell complained.

Polly hung her head.
Meanwhile, Sam was whispering
in the Captain's ear.

"Go below decks please,
Polly," the Captain said quietly. "We need
to discuss what to do with you."

Polly flapped down the stairs and sat on a cannon. After a while she heard sawing and banging up on deck.

What would be her punishment?
Would they make her walk the plank?
Or fly over the plank, perhaps? Then what?

Polly began packing her belongings into a bag.
She didn't have much. A cracked mirror. A bell
that had lost its ring. Half a mouldy cracker.

"You can come up now, Polly," the Captain called. Miserably, Polly flapped her way back up on deck.

What she saw there made her beak drop open. Right in the middle of the deck there stood the most wonderful perch she had ever seen. It had a rain cover, a mirror, a bell and a cracker box.

"Do you like it?" Sam asked. She nodded and flapped up onto the perch. It was padded!

No one had ever been so kind to her before. "I'm sorry I let you down," Polly squawked, shedding a tear. "I'll be a better look-out next time."

"It's us who let you down," the Captain said. "We should have taken better care of you. We didn't think about where you slept at night. We weren't kind to you, and that's why the ship was put in danger."

As the Captain carried on with his speech, the pirates gathered around to inspect the perch. Nell checked her hair in the mirror. Sam rang the little bell. And Polly?

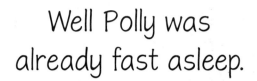

Well Polly was
already fast asleep.

NOTES FOR PARENTS AND TEACHERS

Pirates to the Rescue

The books in the 'Pirates to the Rescue' series are designed to help children recognise the virtues of generosity, honesty, politeness and kindness. Reading these books will show children that their actions and behaviour have a real effect on people around them, helping them to recognise what is right and wrong, and to think about what to do when faced with difficult choices.

Helping Polly Parrot!

'Helping Polly Parrot' is intended to be an engaging and enjoyable read for children aged 4-7. The book will help children recognise why it's important to be kind and that helping others builds relationships and communities.

It's difficult for small children to think of others without gentle reminders or persuasion. Children may struggle to appreciate what exactly is 'in it for them'. The idea of reciprocal giving is an alien concept; that a small act of kindness towards another now might result in a greater, or equivalent kindess in return at a future date, is a hard one for a child to appreciate given that their focus is on the here and now. But with guidance, patience and showing by example, children can, and will, learn to imitate and understand these behaviours in time.

Learning how to be kind helps children to develop relationships with others, to learn how their behaviour affects others, and to understand each other's feelings. Some children find it difficult to think about others. Learning how to help, to give praise to your friends and family are vital skills in developing consideration for others, an essential part of growing up. To have another child give something to you, even if it's just a smile or a hug, is useful for developing self-esteem and helps them learn to express gratitude and develop friendships.

Suggested follow-up activities

When Polly realises she's let the pirates down, her first thought is that the Captain will punish her. She blames herself. The Captain, however, is wise. He recognises that it is, in fact, his own lack of kindness which has led to the problem. Only an unexpected act of kindness towards Polly can rectify the situation.

Ask your child to put him or herself in the position of Polly when she's trying to find a place to sleep. Is it fair that she has to sleep on top of the mast? How does she feel when she wakes to find she's put the ship in danger? Why does the Captain not punish Polly? Would punishing her have brought about the same result? How do the rest of the crew react when Polly is given her own perch?

Take time to explain what kindness is, and why it is important. Don't assume your child will know. Help your child to make gifts, or bake biscuits to give to friends and family. Make a card for someone, telling your child it's to cheer him/her up. Play Doctors and encourage your child to take a caring role over the patients. Emphasise how kindness and caring can help people to get better.

Notice and praise acts of kindness from your child, however minor. Say 'That was very kind to give me a cuddle. I feel much better now.' Or 'You were very kind to share your sweets with your sister.' Use toys to act out scenarios. Isolate one toy and tell your child it is sad and lonely. 'How can we make her feel better?'

Don't forget to be kind to your partner, or older siblings. Make a show of it. Young children watch and imitate adult behaviour. Hold open a door. Or thank someone carefully if they do something nice for you. Tell your child what you are going to do and why. 'I'm going to make Mummy a nice hot drink because she's had a long day.'

BOOKS TO SHARE

A First Look at Setting a Good Example:
I Can Make A Difference
by Pat Thomas and Lesley Harker (Wayland, 2010)

This delightful picture book helps children to understand why it is important to help others and be considerate by setting a good example.

A First Look at Respect for Others: Everyone Matters
by Pat Thomas and Lesley Harker (Wayland, 2010)

This charming book introduces children to the concept of respect. Everyone deserves respect and to be treated fairly. This book describes how you can earn respect, by being polite, honest or listening to others. Readers will also discover how having respect for ourselves and others makes the world a nicer place to be in.

Cowboys Can Be Kind
by Timothy Knapman (QED, 2012)

A humorous and gentle approach to teaching about kindness, written in rhyme.